The Boy Who Grew A Tree

Illustrated by
Sojung Kim-McCarthy

Polly Ho-Yen

Published by Knights Of

Knights Of ltd, Registered Offices: 119 Marylebone Road, London, NW1 5PU

www.knightsof.media

First published in the UK 2022

001

Written by Polly Ho-Yen,

Text and cover copyright © Polly Ho-Yen, 2022

Illustration © Sojung Kim-McCarthy, 2022

Set in Ovo Standard / 14 pt

Typeset by Marssaié Jordan

Design by Marssaié Jordan

Printed and bound in the UK

A CIP catalogue record for this book will be available from the British Library

ISBN: 9781913311308

2 4 6 8 10 9 7 5 3 1

For B and her Babu
And for all the Timis out there.

The days that her grandfather took her to the library were her very favourite.

It was usually on a Sunday, because he played table tennis on Saturdays and she was at school in the week. Sunday was their day.

She'd choose a stack of books and they'd lose themselves in different lands and places. Sometimes they would fly with dragons, on other days they'd be under the sea. Whatever the book though, when she'd finished reading, she always found herself asking him for another story – a story from his head.

Today was no different.

"Tell me Babu," she said, in that direct way she had of speaking and because Babu was her name for him. "Tell me the story about the tree."

She climbed onto his lap and looked at him. Sometimes she could be rather serious.

"The one about the tree and the full moon and the great, big baboon?" her Babu said, his eyes glinting a little.

"No, not that one."

"Ah, the one about the tree and the stone giant and the saxophone?"

"No, no," she said, pretending to be cross even though she knew his game. He always pretended he didn't know, although she asked for the same tale every time. "The one about you!"

Babu had told her that this story was about him.

That it was real.

That he was not even kidding.

"The one about the tree and the library and me?" he asked.

"Yes, that one," she said.

"Well," her Babu said, drawing her close. "There was a boy..."

Chapter 1

There was a boy called Timi who had always liked growing things.

When he was three years old, he'd buried his wellington boot under three pillows and watered it every day until his mum found it.

It hadn't grown into anything. But that didn't put him off.

When he was a little bit older, he collected seeds from apples and grew them in old yoghurt pots on his windowsill. He took a piece of mint from the school garden and let it sit in a glass of water where it grew white root tendrils that looked like hair. He planted it in a patch of soil at the bottom of his block where it grew strong. It came back every year.

His mum would always know where to find him whenever he disappeared off. He'd be in his bedroom, at his windowsill. 'The little garden,' Mum called it.

The 'little garden' was getting bigger. Timi's class had grown bean plants in school, although not everyone had wanted to take one home. But Timi had found a space for them amongst the apple seedlings.

Mum's tummy looked like an apple these days. It was round and hard and domed but sometimes it would move.

"There's the baby," Mum would say when Timi would spot the little movements in her tummy.

Timi imagined the baby to be like one of his seedlings. Starting so very tiny but over time, a root would push its way out of the seed, a little leaf would uncoil. And then another and another and the stalk would grow strong and green, up and up.

It was almost impossible to believe that the tall bean plant in front of him had started off as just a shiny, speckled seed that he could hold in the palm of his hand.

And it was almost as impossible to believe that there really was a baby in his Mum's tummy.

Chapter 2

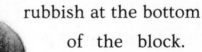

Timi noticed things that would pass most people by. Though he lived in a city, surrounded by buildings and roads and cars and buses, he spotted nature everywhere.

He would see the furry caterpillar on the leaf of a bush by the bus stop. Or the spider's web on the pile of rubbish at the bottom of the block.

He knew which rocks in the little patch of grass by the playground would have long pink worms beneath them, and the one which hid the most scuttling woodlice.

But he wasn't, perhaps, very good at noticing people.

He had been digging with a stick in the outside space at the after-school club, quite lost in his thoughts, when he heard a voice.

"What are you doing?"

It took Timi a moment to realise that the voice was speaking to him.

He looked up. A girl and a boy were standing over him. They were both just a little older than him. He didn't recognise them. They must go to a different school, he thought.

"Just looking," he said. He glanced around the small yard they were in. It was his first time at the after-school club and

he didn't know anyone there. He hadn't
realised anyone had been watching him.

He hoped they wouldn't ask him anymore
but the girl said: "Looking for what?"

Timi glanced down at the dark red beetle
pupa that he had just discovered in the
ground. He didn't find beetle pupa that
often – the time when an insect is changing

and grows a shiny skin before it emerges as a grown-up beetle. Lots of people knew about caterpillars, cocoons and butterflies, but not so much about a beetle pupa. It was precious and he didn't trust the girl and boy not to hurt it.

Timi had seen it time and time again; people hurting small things, even when they didn't mean to. They'd tread on the daisies that were trying to spring up in the grass in the park, they'd brush away a tiny spider that landed on their arm without noticing what it was, they'd step on the snail that was winding its way across the pavement. The list was endless. He carefully put the piece of mud that was hiding the pupa back down on the ground.

"Nothing. Just, you know – buried treasure." It was not really a lie, Timi thought.

"Buried treasure. You'll be lucky to find anything here," the boy said, kicking at the ground. Now that Timi was looking at the boy, he saw that the toes of his shoes were peeling away from the soles. He wondered if he'd worn them out by kicking at the ground like he had just done. And when he looked up, he saw the boy had dark, fuzzy hair that stuck out in strands and looked not unlike the shape of the tiny, coiled pupa.

"We haven't seen you here before," the girl said. She, Timi noticed, had tiny felt-tip drawings on her hands. It looked like they were pictures of the waves of the sea or maybe it was just a pretty pattern – but it made Timi think of the dapples in a puddle just after you jumped in it.

"Have you been here before?" the girl spoke again, and Timi tried to pull his eyes from the drawings on her hands.

"I've just started," Timi replied.

He didn't really understand why he'd begun coming to the after school club. His mum had just told him that it was happening. She didn't seem to hear Timi when he'd asked her why.

Her tummy had got so much bigger in the last few weeks. She could only walk very slowly now, and she was always tired.

"What's your name?" the boy asked.

"Timi."

"You can come with us," the girl said.

"Come where?" Timi asked.

But then one of the adults shouted out to them that someone had come to pick them up. They ran away, before Timi could even find out their names.

Chapter 3

Abi and Mo.

That was what the girl and boy were called.

Timi saw them the next day after school. They were with some other children, who were also a bit older than him.

"That's Timi," Abi said when they saw him. Timi spotted that today she had curly lines drawn onto her hands in pink and blue. It made him think of the spiral of a snail shell, which was one of those things that Timi could look at for a really long time.

Some of the other kids muttered hello to him. He looked over at them briefly and spotted a collection of things about them: one of them had laces undone that were trailing from their shoe, reminding Timi of snake skins left lying on the ground. He'd never seen a snakeskin in real life, but he'd learned about them in school. Another boy had large deep, brown eyes that glowed like pebbles after it had been raining. A girl wore a headscarf and Timi noticed thar she rubbed the fabric of it very gently between her thumb and finger when she talked.

He had a strange kind of feeling. It was

two things at the same time: he wanted to be alone and yet he wanted to be with them too.

"We're thinking of breaking in to the library," Mo said.

"How are we going to get in?" the kid with the undone shoelaces asked.

"I know the code to the door," Abi said. "My mum worked there."

"But it's closed down," said the brown-eyed boy. He really did have big eyes. But they looked worried now.

"So what?" Abi asked.

"It's haunted too, you know," said Mo to the boy with big eyes.

Timi knew the library that they were talking about. It had shut down a few weeks ago. It was quite an old building that had red bricks and white stone patterns around the windows. Timi had spotted before that some of the bricks had lichen growing over them – a kind of fungus that looked pale green and grew in patches.

He'd walked past the library with his mum a couple of days ago and saw the door was shut and the lights weren't on. The windows looked like dark pools and it seemed even older somehow, like that – all closed up with no lights on.

"Are you afraid of ghosts?" Mo said to the big-eyed boy. He stood in a way that made him look much taller as he spoke. Timi thought that he could see his spine unfurling like a beanstalk would rising up from its seed.

"I'll go in," said the boy, although his voice sounded quiet.

"What about you, Timi?" Abi asked. "Will you go in?"

Timi thought about his mum telling him this morning that he was going to get collected from the club by his auntie.

She said that he would probably have to stay overnight with his auntie, too. They needed to do some checks on her and the baby at the hospital.

You stay with your auntie.

You be a good boy.

"I'll go in," Timi said.

Chapter 4

Chapter 4

A week later, Timi was standing in front of the locked-up entrance of the library. He didn't know if it was really haunted, but he still felt scared about going in there.

He knew it wasn't the right thing to do, even though Abi said that she knew that it was safe because she'd heard her mum talking about it.

"They're going to pull it down and make flats here, Mum says," Abi said. "There was a protest but Mum said people don't care enough."

The front door of the library looked tall and black like a shadow. Mo and Abi led everyone round to the back of the building to a smaller door. As Timi passed the bricks that had the patch of the ghostly green lichen, he reached out to stroke it ever so gently. There were a few of the kids from the after-school club and some others that Timi hadn't seen before so he stayed near the back of the group.

He wasn't really sure what they were going to do when they got in but, despite his worries, he felt drawn to being there. Whether it was because he wanted to be with Abi and Mo or that he wanted to prove that he wasn't afraid (of anything), he wasn't sure.

It was easier getting away now that he was staying with his auntie too. If he'd been at home with Mum then she wouldn't have let him come out by himself. But his mum was still in hospital. The baby had come early, too early. She was strong, his mum told him on the phone, but she needed help to do all the things that you can normally do on your own – like keeping warm and eating - and so he needed to stay with his auntie until the baby could come home.

Timi hadn't been sure that he would be able to get away to meet Abi and Mo, but it turned out not to be a problem. It was the weekend and he went with his older cousins to the shops. He told them that he was going to meet some friends and they let him slip away. It was almost too easy.

Abi punched the buttons of the silver keypad on the door. Timi was standing close enough to see her do it, and saw that the code made a pattern like a zig-zag line going downwards.

The door opened soundlessly.

Inside, it looked murky and still.

"Who's first?" Mo said.

There was a moment when no one spoke or moved. Even Abi didn't step forward.

"You first," said Abi to the big-eyed boy who had come along in the end, although Timi thought he looked like he really didn't want to be there. He kept twisting his hands together and looking all around him.

"I don't know," the big-eyed boy said.

"You said that you would go in," said Mo.

The boy peered into the open door of the

library. Timi looked round him. There was a shadowy corridor, and a stale smell in the air.

"I – I..." the boy said.

"I'll go in," Timi said and, before anyone could stop him, he stepped around the boy and walked down the corridor.

He thought that the others would follow him but, as he made his way to the main room of the building, where the books would be, he realised that he was alone.

The library was silence and dust. The shelves were bare, apart from a few books that had been left behind in wonky piles. Some other things had not been tidied away – a little box of coloured strips of paper, some flyers for something Timi couldn't make out - but mostly the room had been emptied.

The curtains were closed, but there was a small gap where they hadn't been pulled together properly. Through the gap, a ray of afternoon sunlight poured in..

Timi overheard Mo say something that he couldn't quite hear. Then there was a scuffle, a burst of voices and suddenly the door slammed shut. Timi heard footsteps and then, someone shouting.

The door opened again. Timi shrank behind one of the bookcases as he saw a man, that was definitely not Abi or Mo or the big-eyed boy, looking round the library. He took a few steps in. Timi held his breath and tried not to make even the smallest of sounds.

Then the man turned away and went back through the door and out into the sunshine.

The door slammed shut.

Timi looked around him. He knew he shouldn't be in there and wanted to leave but, while the man was still close by, he thought that he should wait for a little while to be sure that he had gone.

There was another part of him too, that didn't want to go back to a place that was not his home. He had not spoken to his mum that day and he wondered how his little sister was, who he had never met.

The ray of light through the curtain had grown stronger in the time that Timi had been there. The criss-cross pattern of the wooden floor was almost glowing from the light shining in.

If Timi had been any other boy in the world, then he would almost certainly not have spotted it.

In the light, in the narrow gap between the floorboards, a tiny, green seedling was surging up.

❧ Chapter 5 ❧

It was as delicate as a snowflake.

The seedling was so brightly green that it seemed to Timi he could almost see through it.

He knelt down to the floor to look at it closely and examined its tiny, thin stalk and its two baby leaves.

He knew better than to try and touch it. It was fragile and, being so small, just a rough touch could damage it. But he also knew that, like his seedlings in his 'little garden', it would need to be watered to grow. There was no chance of it being able to get any rain inside the library. For a moment he thought of his seedlings at home, and wondered if Mum would've remembered to tell someone to water them. He'd been away from his little pots for so long, they would become dried out by now.

He looked around the empty library and carefully went back to the hallway he'd come through. There were several doors leading off the corridor. He tried one and found an old store cupboard. The next was a toilet. But the one after that was a kitchen.

A cup lay abandoned in the sink. Timi filled it to the brim and carried it through into the library.

He couldn't see any soil through the floorboards. It seemed unbelievable that the seedling had sprung up here in this tiny crack.

But Timi had seen plants growing out of the cracks between bricks. Moss that covered tarmac. It wasn't impossible that somehow this seedling had grown here. Just very, very unusual.

Timi poured the water carefully into the crack between the floorboards at the bottom of the thin stalk, taking care not to let the stream damage the tiny seedling.

"There you are," he whispered to it.

The sun seemed to shine more brightly for a minute. The seedling looked greener than ever.

Chapter 6

The next day, at the after-school club, Abi ran straight over to Timi. "What happened?" she asked him. "We didn't see you come out. Someone spotted us so we ran away."

Timi didn't want to tell the older kids about the seedling and, since the moment they'd tried to force the big-eyed boy to go into the library, he didn't want to spend time with them anymore either.

"Nothing happened," he said.

"Mo thinks it's too dangerous to go back," Abi said. "We thought that we'd find somewhere else. There's a spot in the park that's surrounded by trees but there's a hole in the bushes that you can make your way into."

"What do you want to do there?" Timi asked. He was curious.

"I don't know," Abi admitted. "Just have a place of our own, I guess. Do you want to come? To the park?"

"I have to stay home to help my mum," Timi said. "I've got a baby sister."

"Oh, a baby," Abi said. "I like babies." She danced away from him.

Timi wasn't sure that he liked babies. He hadn't been telling the truth: his mum was still in hospital and he still hadn't met Bisi, his baby sister. She had a name now, which made Timi feel like he knew her a little, although the truth was that he didn't know her at all.

The only thing that was making Timi feel just a tiny bit better about everything was the thought of the seedling in the library.

He'd decided that he would go back.

On his own.

He was going to check that it was OK.

It wasn't difficult to slip away again.

He was still at his auntie's house while his mum stayed in hospital. His auntie thought that his cousins were looking after for him and his cousins thought that he was with his friends.

The first time that he made it back to the library, he made sure that he looked all around for anyone that might be watching the entrance. He waited, hidden behind a dark green bush just to be extra careful. There was no sign of the man that he'd seen before. Then he ran towards the door and punched in the code that he'd seen Abi enter, closing the door quickly behind him.

The air was so still in the library that for a moment it made Timi still himself. He stayed there, standing by the door, just to be sure that no one had seen him come in. When a minute passed, he waited for a few moments more in the peace. It felt good to be there. Timi felt something unknot inside him.

Then, remembering why he'd come there, he walked into the bigger room of the library where he'd found the seedling.

Straightaway, he stopped in his tracks.

The seedling was still there.

Only it had grown bigger. Much, much bigger.

It was already as tall as Timi and had sprouted leaves and off-shoots. It was still remarkably green, almost glowing with green.

Timi reached out for one of its leaves, which felt both soft and strong at the same time.

"How did you do that?" he asked it.

Timi knew that the plant wouldn't answer

him back with words, but he'd found with his seedlings in his little garden that if he spoke to them, it felt like they were answering him back somehow. Not with words but more like with a feeling that they had heard him.

The little seedling seemed to answer him back in that way, and Timi nodded.

He went back to the kitchen and filled up the cup he had used before.

He watered the crack in the floorboards that the stalk was surging through. The crack had grown bigger since the last time he'd been here too.

He knew that it would need more than one cup; he went back to the kitchen three times in total before he felt that it had had enough water.

Timi spoke again to the plant: "I don't know how you did that."

As he turned to leave, he made it almost

to the door before he ran back to check that the seedling was really there, that it had grown as much as it had.

It just couldn't be real, he thought, even though he'd just seen it seconds ago. Nothing could grow that fast. But, when he returned to it, it was as green and tall and strong as he remembered.

Chapter 7

Timi knew something wasn't right with this growing seedling.

Things didn't grow that quickly.

They couldn't.

The thought of that bright green plant stayed with him. It grew into his dreams. Giant leaves unfurled in his mind, but, when he woke up, he was still at his auntie's house and she had no plants in her flat at all.

He thought again about his little garden, but his auntie said she was too busy to take him over and he didn't have a key to get in by himself.

But he could return to the library. He still felt unsure that he was remembering it right, that the seedling had grown so much. Perhaps it had just been a dream. Could he have only imagined it? Because a plant couldn't grow that much in just a few days. Timi felt sure about that.

A couple of days later, Timi returned to the library.

He heard it almost as soon as he opened the door, as a breeze swept down the corridor and rustled the leaves. It was now no longer a seedling, no longer a plant... it was a tree.

It had a trunk that felt strong to touch, and had grown thick and brown. Branches had started to form and leaves grew in clusters upon them.

Timi could feel his own heartbeat all of a sudden. It felt like it was not just in his chest

but in his whole body: his head, his ears, his arms and stomach. Every part of him seemed to pulse at seeing the strangeness of it: this little tree that had grown all by itself in the middle of a closed-down library with just four cups of water.

He counted the days from when he had first seen the tiny seedling, on that first trip to the library with the others. It had only been one, two, three, four, five, six days! It was impossible that the seedling could have become a tree in so short a time.

But Timi reached for the trunk and it felt solid beneath his hand. He gently tickled the leaves, which glowed green in the ray of sunlight that was still inching in through the crack between the curtains.

He'd need something bigger than a cup to water it now. And he'd need to find a way to open one of the curtains at the top.

Timi understood how important it was for plants to have water and light. They needed attention too, he thought. He was trying not to think of his apple seedlings and the wandering bean plants that would almost definitely not have survived being unwatered for so long.

There wasn't anything suitable in the kitchen, but in one of the cupboards Timi found an old bucket and he filled it with as much water as he could carry.

"How's that?" he asked the tree as he fed it the water.

As before, it didn't answer him with any words but there was a feeling in the air that made Timi sure it was answering him back; thank you.

 Chapter 8

One week from when he had discovered the tree, Timi tried to speak to his baby sister Bisi. But, unlike the tree, he wasn't able to give her what she needed, and she showed no signs of having heard him. Her little fists pawed the air and then her face screwed up as she began to cry.

Mum and Bisi had come home from hospital now. Timi thought he'd feel better now they were back, but, in an odd kind of way, he felt even lonelier than he did before. He was with his mum and Bisi more now, but his mum was so tired that he still had to go and stay with his auntie a lot. And Bisi was so small that there wasn't much that she could do; all she seemed to want was to be with their mum.

"It won't be long before she'll want to play with you," Mum said, bundling Bisi to her. "She'll grow up before you know it. You can teach her all the things you know."

Timi thought his mum might talk about his little garden and that he might be able to share that with Bisi, but she didn't mention it.

It might have been, Timi thought, because he'd been asking every day for another small bag of compost. All of his plants had died from not being watered and he needed to start over again. He'd emptied out all the pots and washed them, ready to go. All he needed now was some compost. He already had some seeds he'd saved that he could use. But there was always a reason why they couldn't go to the shop to get it. Yesterday they'd got close to leaving, but then Bisi had needed feeding again and, by the time she'd finished and had her nappy changed, it was Timi's bedtime.

Then, Mum said that she needed Timi to be really, really good.

He needed to go stay with his other auntie over the holidays, who lived across the city. The auntie who had been looking after him had family coming to visit, but Mum still needed some help.

Timi had to go somewhere else for the time being.

"Why can't I stay with you?" Timi asked. "I can help you look after Bisi."

"I just need a bit more time," his mum said. "To recover. Then we'll all be together again. It's just a short stay during the holidays, I promise. It'll be over before you know it."

It was a long journey. His other auntie came to collect him. They had to take three different buses and, as Timi sat on the hard seat that felt a bit like carpet, clutching his small bag of clothes to his lap, he felt very far from his home, his mum and Bisi. His auntie looked out the window and occasionally pointed things out to him. The buildings looked different to Timi. It was part of the city that he'd never been to before and, though he'd lived here his whole life, it seemed as strange to him as if he were in a different country.

He knew he wouldn't be able to return to the library and the tree while he stayed with this auntie. Maybe by the time he came back home, the library would have been knocked down to make way for the flats. Abi had talked about that happening on that first day they went there. And, even if the library was still there, how would the tree survive without water? It would need it more than ever now that it had grown so much bigger.

Without Timi, it wouldn't be able to flourish.

He had a little bed on the floor of the room he was sharing with his auntie's son. His name was Isaac and he was a couple of years younger than Timi. He reminded Timi a little of the big-eyed boy who had been afraid, except Isaac had nothing to be afraid of and he smiled easily and laughed often.

He wanted Timi to play with him all the time, which was nice in a way, although Timi felt himself missing the stillness of the library and wondering, wondering whether the tree was still growing without him.

Chapter 9

At the beginning, the holidays didn't pass quickly, as his mum had told him they would. Timi looked at the calendar in the kitchen every day, counting the number of nights until school would start again and he would go home.

The things that he mostly noticed at his auntie's house were the sounds in the kitchen. His auntie loved to cook and, as she threw things into a pan, the heat and steam and the bubbling and the spitting made Timi think that the whole kitchen was alive, as though it were a dragon breathing fire and lashing its tail.

They didn't go out very often, but there was a big window that looked down onto a largish park and at first Timi spent most of his time there, gazing down at the patch of the grass and the curly shapes of the tree leaves from above. He thought about his tree in the library and he also found himself imagining all the things that he might do if he were in that park. Perhaps he would feel the tips of the blades of the grass on his palm, so that it would tickle him. Maybe he would listen to the rustling sound the leaves would make when they were swayed by a breeze. He would grow quiet, sitting there at the window, by himself, imagining he was somewhere else.

But then Isaac, who loved building things, started to make the biggest tower he could, in the corner of the sitting room, and Timi got drawn into helping him. They used plastic bricks at the base and when they ran out they turned to bits of cardboard that his auntie was going to put into the recycling. They had to stand on chairs to add more to it and then, when they couldn't reach, even when they stood on a chair, Isaac's older sister and his dad joined in too. They worked on it every day and soon, without Timi realising it, the tower was skimming the ceiling and there was only one day left before he would be returning home.

"We did it," Isaac said proudly, but Timi's auntie said it was an eyesore. Isaac asked her what that meant and she said that it made her eye feel sore, that was what an eyesore was.

"Oh," Isaac said. "Well, I still like it."

Isaac insisted that it was solid, but everyone still walked past the tower very carefully in case it fell down.

He cried when Timi left and wouldn't let go of his leg. He wanted to come on the long bus journey with them, but Timi's auntie asked him who would take care of the tower if both he and Timi were gone and so Isaac stayed behind.

It seemed far longer than two weeks since he and his auntie had made the journey across the city, and Timi felt different inside to how he had when he'd sat on the bus on the way over. He was sad to say goodbye to Isaac and he wondered how long his auntie would let him keep the tower up

in the sitting room. When he asked her, she chuckled and said: "I'll give him one afternoon."

Timi didn't like to imagine Isaac with his tower gone, and was unsure of when he might see him again, but he was looking forward to seeing his mum. And Bisi too. Maybe she'd grown like the tree had – all in one go – and so she'd be able to play with him now and she wouldn't just cry for milk.

And he wanted to see the tree in the library, of course.

He wanted to know if it had grown too.

Chapter 10

The library was still standing, Timi noticed with relief, when he first managed to get away from his cousins.

His mum had been wrong about them spending more time together now, and wrong about Bisi wanting to talk to him. He still went to the after-school club and spent a few nights every week with his auntie who lived close by.

The only good thing about this was that it was easy to slip away from his cousins again.

The door of the library felt a little

stiffer than it had before. Timi had to lean his weight against it to open it. When he was inside, there was a moment when he was sure that the tree wasn't there but, as he walked into the main room, he saw that it was, and was as tall as it was when he'd last visited, although no bigger.

It was still standing but it looked grey. Its leaves were dull and they drooped on the branches. One strong gust of wind might

whip them from the tree for good. The trunk looked almost sagging, leaning to one side ever so slightly as though it were tired.

'I'm sorry, I'm sorry," Timi whispered to the tree urgently as he tipped a bucket of water into the crack. He hoped that the tree might start to look better immediately but it continued to look withered and weak. It didn't even seem to Timi like it was talking back to him anymore, but he spoke to it anyway.

"Do you need more?" he asked it.

He filled the bucket again and gave it another long drink. Then he went to the window on the side of the library that was not by the road, so people wouldn't be able to look in, and pulled the curtain open a bit more, so more light fell onto its branches. The curtain was stuck at first but Timi tugged at it until he managed to pull it open wide.

The sun's rays filled the room and when Timi looked back at the tree he thought that it already looked a little bit greener than it had when he first came in.

"Are you feeling better?" Timi asked the tree. "Have you had enough to drink?"

The way he'd always been able to tell with one of his pots in his little garden if they'd had enough water, was by feeling the soil to see if it felt damp and looked black with moisture. But here in the library, he couldn't see any soil, just the criss-cross of the floorboards.

He laid his hand against the floorboards at the base of the trunk. They felt damp from the last bucket of water and so Timi trusted that the tree had had enough. Also, he promised himself, he would be back tomorrow to check on it.

Chapter 11

The next day when Timi returned to the library, the tree had grown a full metre overnight. Timi could no longer even touch the top of it.

He only had a little bit of time before he was due back at his auntie's for dinner, so he spent most of his time in the library lugging buckets of water from the kitchen to the tree, until he felt satisfied that the tree had had enough to drink.

"I'll come back again soon," he told it before he left. He felt calmer seeing that the tree had not only grown but looked as healthy as it did before the holidays when he had gone away.

He had the feeling that the tree was answering him back now, acknowledging that it would see him again soon. He crept from the library and stole away back to his auntie's house.

The next time that he came back, the tree had grown another metre and was taller than the empty bookshelves.

The time after that, it had grown not only taller but wider as well. Its branches reached outwards and, standing beneath it, Timi felt like he was under a green, leafy umbrella.

He always did the same thing every time he was at the library. He watered the tree with the bucket, he opened up the curtain to give it light and he spoke to it a little. Timi had the same feeling of wonder watching the tree growing in the library as he did when he saw one of his apple seedings sprouting. The seedlings at home grew much more

slowly, but it still seemed like a miracle to watch a leaf unfurl and get strong under his care, and for another and another to appear.

But this tree was something else. Like on the first day that he had spotted its growth spurt, he still felt like he needed to keep coming back to check that it was really there. It continued to seem impossible.

But it was always there. Always growing.

Chapter 12

One day, a few weeks after the holiday when Timi had stayed with his auntie and Isaac, he was on his way to the library to visit the tree when he spotted Abi and Mo on the street. They had not spoken to Timi much since he had said that he wasn't going to come with them to the park that time.

They were across the road from him, with some other kids. They walked so closely together that it was hard to tell them apart. Timi heard one of them yell something loudly, but he didn't look over at them.

He shrank against the shopfront and hoped that they hadn't seen him. When he was sure that they would have passed him, he glanced across the road and saw that they had disappeared down the street.

He needed to get to the library to see the tree. It had been a few days since he'd been able to get away.

Timi still looked around carefully like he had done the first time he came to the library on his own. He didn't spot anyone and when he went in, closing the door behind him, he felt a sense of calm rush over him as he walked over to the tree.

The trunk was thick and strong now, and textured so that Timi could fit his fingers into the pattern of holes upon the bark. He patted it and then went to the kitchen to fill the bucket.

He was lugging the first bucket of water back to the tree when he heard the sound of the door handle opening. He wasn't sure what to do – whether to let the water fall from the bucket and pour out across the floor, or to hide, or what. So, he ended up freezing, the bucket in his hand, standing still exactly where he was.

"What are you doing?" said a voice that Timi recognised immediately. It was the same question that she'd asked him when she had first met him at the after-school club.

Abi was at the door with Mo and the other kids from the street.

All staring at him, while the bucket of water slipped from his hand and the water hit the floor with a splash.

Chapter 13

Timi's first instinct was to look towards the tree. Though he'd felt the solidity of the trunk beneath his palm and had felt the silkiness of its leaves, he still found it hard to believe that it really existed. Now, with other people here, would it still be there?

He looked towards it.

It hadn't grown much taller in his last few visits, although it had grown many more branches and each branch was flourishing with leaves.

"What... is... that?" Abi said. He looked over at the group; they all looked the same as each other, their mouths hanging open in astonishment.

Timi felt himself flooded with another feeling as they stepped towards the tree; what if they hurt it, what if they told someone about it and it got chopped down? What if he wouldn't be able to protect it?

"It's a... tree," Timi said, although that was quite obvious.

"But how did it get here?"

"It wasn't here before."

"How did it grow?"

Everyone spoke at the same time. Timi couldn't make out who was saying what.

They all looked towards him for answers.

"It's just grown really, really quickly," Timi said. "I saw it on the first day that we were here and from then, it's just gotten bigger and bigger."

There were more mutters: It can't have. Trees don't grow that fast. Someone must have just put it there.

Then, Timi noticed that the big-eyed boy from before was with them and he was kneeling at the base of the tree, examining how the trunk had sprouted out from between the floorboards.

"It's not in a pot, it's growing out of the floorboards. He's telling the truth," the big-eyed boy said.

Abi bent down to look too, and then she reached out and lay her hand across the trunk as if she, like Timi, wanted to touch it to trust that it was really there.

"It's real," she said.

The other children copied Abi, laying a hand onto the trunk and, for just a moment, they were all touching the tree at the same time.

"What have you been doing here?" Abi asked.

"Just watering it," Timi said. "Keeping an eye on it. I think... I think that it likes having company."

"Well, it's got more of us now," said Abi. Later Timi thought that he must have imagined it, but as Abi spoke, he thought that he saw one of the branches burst with greenness as if leaves were sprouting before their eyes.

 Chapter 14

They took it in turns visiting the library to water the tree. It needed more than ever now that it was so big. The day after Abi, Mo, Marcus (that was the name of the big-eyed boy) and the others saw the tree, it grew more than it had ever done before. In every direction.

"It's going to get too big for the library soon," Abi said. Timi looked up at the branches and knew that she was right.

"Has your mum said anything more about the library being replaced with flats?" he asked her.

"No. But I could ask her," Abi said.

"If that goes ahead, then there will be nothing to protect the tree," Timi said.

"We'll have to think of a way of stopping them," said Marcus.

"How will we be able to stop them?" asked Mo.

"We'll have to find a way," said Timi.

They'd been coming to the library at every moment they could, and the tree had started

to change shape so it
was easy for them
to climb amongst
the branches.

During that
conversation
they had all
been sitting on a
different branch, surrounded by leaves as if
they were in their own private den.

Before they left that night, Marcus and
Timi filled buckets while Abi and Mo took
them through to the tree. Marcus and Mo
had brought buckets they'd
found at home and so it was
easier to water it now if
they did it together.

"Is that enough water?
Can I help?" Roberta
asked Timi. Roberta was

the girl with the headscarf who liked to feel the fabric in her fingers. Timi noticed that she stroked the leaves of the tree in much the same way as she felt her headscarf, and she'd been doing that as they'd watered it.

Timi looked towards the tree and silently asked it if it was OK.

"I think it's fine," Timi said with a smile.

Chapter 15

The following day, Abi ran over to Timi as soon as he got to the after-school club.

"Timi, the demolition team – they're going to the library tomorrow," she said. Marcus and Mo had run over too. All of their faces looked sad, their eyes barely lifting from the ground.

"Tomorrow? When?" Timi was aware of his heart beating loudly inside him.

"I don't know, I guess that it might be first thing, but they could come anytime," Abi answered.

"Are you sure it's tomorrow?" Timi asked. He felt it, like a pain in his chest, that he was not there with the tree, protecting it.

"That's what my mum said."

"We've got to get there," he said.

"I know," said Abi.

"But what are we even going to do?" asked Mo.

"Maybe that's all that we need to do," said Marcus. "We just need to be there. We need to be there and not leave. They won't be able to demolish the library if we refuse to go."

"They'll make us leave, call the police," said Mo.

"Maybe they will," Marcus said. "But we'll

keep sending more kids to go in and protect it. We could message everyone we know and make people keep arriving, all of the time."

"That's crazy," said Mo.

"But it could work," said Abi, placing both her hands on her hips. Timi spotted that she had drawn faces on her hands that day. It felt like they were almost watching him.

"Maybe when they see the tree," Timi said, "they won't want to do it. Once they see the tree and we tell them what it's like, they'll want to protect it too."

"Maybe," said Abi, but she didn't sound very convinced.

"We've got to try," Timi said.

The first challenge they had was leaving the after-school club without any of the adults stopping them.

But that turned out not to be very difficult.

When the adults were talking to a parent who had just arrived and they were all looking the other way, the group of kids slipped through the open door and out into the street.

Timi could feel his heart beating hard in his chest again as they ran from the building, waiting for a shout from behind them, but no one was following them. For those few minutes, they had not been noticed. Before any more time went by, they were already running away from the club – out of earshot of anyone who might have spotted them.

They sprinted all the way to the library, and it was only when the door slammed behind them did Timi feel that he could take a full breath.

They crowded into the room where the tree was growing. Since the last time they had been there, it had grown enormously.

Massive branches had sprouted from its trunk and were almost touching the walls. Timi felt like all he could see was green.

Abi swung up easily onto one of the lower branches and climbed onto a spot where she could sit against the trunk. Each of the other children followed her up until the tree was holding all of them.

"It's grown so much since you've all been here," Timi said.

Mo was flicking through the pile of books that had been left behind and looked around at him.

"It grew a lot when it was just you coming here," he said back.

"But it's huge now," Timi said. "And that's been since we've all been here. I think it likes more people being around it."

"You said that before," Abi said. "That the tree likes this or likes that – how do you know?"

"I don't really know," Timi admitted. "I just have the feeling that it does."

They both looked around at the tree. The children looked as though they were birds settling down to roost amongst the branches.

"You know," Abi said. "I think we might need to get more people. My family is quite big..."

Timi remembered Abi saying that she liked babies.

"How many brothers and sisters do you have?" he asked.

"Four," she said. "I've got a baby sister and two little brothers and an older sister. I'm the second oldest." As she spoke, she pointed out little faces she'd drawn on her fingers and wiggled them in turn. Timi saw that they all had upturned smiles for mouths.

"And you like them – your brothers and sisters?" asked Timi.

Abi thought about that for a minute or two. "They're my brothers and sisters," she said. "They're just... I mean sometimes I think I don't like them but they're always there, you know. How many brothers and sisters do you have?"

"Just my sister who's a baby," said Timi.

"Just the two of you," Abi said. "That's special."

"Is it?" Timi asked.

"Well, you just have each other to look out for. My mum says that me and my brothers and sisters have to look out for each other and because there's so many of us, that's easy to do. If there's just two of you, you only have each other. But at least you've got each other."

Timi thought again about the small scrunched up face of Bisi. She still seemed so small. It would be a long time before she would be able to speak to him but until then, he could look after her, just like Abi said. Maybe one day, Bisi would look after him too.

He remembered then that there had been a time when he'd been excited to meet her, and his mum had spoken to him about how it was going to be different because she was coming but that it was going to be OK. He had been a bit nervous about it, but mostly excited. He'd forgotten that he'd felt like that.

For a moment he wished that Bisi was there so that he could show her the tree. Then he remembered the reason that they were there; the demolition team were coming in the morning.

"Do you really think that we'll be able to stop them?" he asked. But Abi had wandered away and he realised he was talking to himself, or perhaps he was talking to the tree again.

He looked up at the branches but he didn't hear any reply.

Chapter 16

It was a long night in the library. The shadows of the tree grew tall and distorted against the walls. At first the walls were painted with the fading light of the day but then as night fell, it was the yellow glow of the streetlights.

Noises from the street seemed louder than Timi had ever heard them. He was sure that he wouldn't be able to sleep.

The other children had crept down from the tree when they needed to rest and settled at the base of the trunk, amongst the curves of the floorboards that bowed and rose from the roots that were pushing up beneath them.

But Timi stayed in the tree. His back was perfectly arched against a branch, and he couldn't stop imagining how curled up Bisi's body would become when she'd sink, asleep, in his mother's arms.

Mum. She'd be worried about where he was. It wasn't difficult to imagine her face. She might be very cross when she finally did find Timi again.

Where would she think he was? He hadn't told her anything about the library of course and so she would have no idea he was here. He felt a sickness stir in his stomach when he thought about all the things she might be thinking.

Everyone else was asleep but Timi. He could hear their breathing – a gentle rhythm that made him think of waves and it was as if the tree itself was a boat, carrying him off somewhere.

At some point he must have fallen asleep because the next thing he knew, Mo was shouting his name and the room was full of voices - not just the voices of the children - that were shouting all around him.

Chapter 17

There was a very red-faced man who looked like he might pop at any moment. He was wearing a yellow fluorescent vest and had a thick furry moustache. It reminded Timi of one of the caterpillars that he might find munching upon a leaf. It quivered as he shouted.

"Get them out of here," he was yelling to some other workmen. Behind the bustle, Timi also spotted that there were people who were not part of the demolition team.

"Abi!" cried a woman, who had a giant bun and colourful scarf tying it up. She was crying a little bit and ran towards Abi.

Timi wasn't sure if she was angry or cross by the tone of her voice,

but as soon as she reached Abi, she flung her arms around her in a tight hug.

Then Timi realised that e v e r y o n e else's parents were there too. They scooped up

Mo and Marcus and Roberta and the others, so fixed on them that they didn't seem to notice the huge tree that loomed over them all.

And then, through the din, a cry cut through that Timi knew instantly in his bones. It was a tiny little bleating wail. Bisi was there, in the arms of his mum who was looking at him with her eyes glazed with tears.

"Timi, what's going on?" she asked him.

"It's the tree," Timi said.

He turned towards it, wondering, once again, if it might disappear now that there were more people there to see it.

"The tree?" his mum repeated. "The tree!"

Her voice filled with wonder and, when he looked at her again, she was still crying but the tears looked different. They weren't sad tears; they'd changed to look like they were tears of amazement.

"Timi, what's happened here?" she asked.

The other parents were staring up at the tree now too.

"It just... grew," Timi answered her.

He could hear the other children's voices bubbling up all around him.

"Timi's been looking after it," he heard Marcus say. "That's when it started."

"We reckon it's the fastest growing tree in the world," Mo said.

"Now we all look after it," said Abi.

Abi's mum placed a hand against the trunk of the tree, just as Timi had done, and the other children when they had first seen it.

"How could this have happened?" she said very quietly. She turned towards the other parents. "This wasn't here when we closed the library three months ago."

There was another explosion of voices. Timi couldn't hear what they were all saying, but everyone seemed to be disagreeing with each other.

One voice rose over the others. The man in the vest, with the moustache.

"It doesn't matter – we are carrying on, regardless. We'll call someone in to get this chopped down in no time and then the work will continue."

"No," shouted Timi. His voice came from somewhere deep inside of him. It was loud and strong and made everyone stop talking. "You can't chop the tree down. We won't let you."

He looked towards the other children and they all began to climb the branches, scrambling up quickly as if they were a troop of monkeys and had lived among the treetops their whole lives.

Timi was the last to climb up and he turned towards where his mum was standing, with Bisi.

"You too," he said. "Bisi – she needs to be up here too."

His mum hesitated for a moment, but then she passed Bisi carefully to Timi where he sat on the branch. It had been a while since he had held her and he was surprised to notice that she had grown much more than he'd realised in the last few weeks. Her eyes were open and they gazed into the canopy of leaves above her.

"All this," Timi whispered to her. "This is for you too."

Bisi locked eyes with Timi. Her mouth twitched and then settled into a smile: her very first smile.

"She likes it," Timi said to the others.

Abi called for her brothers and sister who scrambled out of reach of their parents and started to climb the tree too. Marcus helped his little brother up and Mo's older sisters

came over too and suddenly the tree was full of more people than Timi had ever seen.

"Everyone," Timi said and looked towards the parents who seemed unsure of where to stand and what to do. Some of them had taken a few steps back when the man with the moustache had started shouting, but others looked longingly towards the tree and the children.

Timi's mum looked at Timi. "Did you really look after this tree?" she said.

Timi shrugged. It hadn't felt like looking after. That seemed too much like work, something you felt you had to do. Coming to see the tree and watering it was more like something Timi couldn't not have done.

"I just came in to see it and watered it. That's all I did," he said. "And then it just grew and grew and grew..."

His mum gazed up towards the branches that were almost resting against the top of the ceiling.

"It's... it's... incredible," she said. "How could this have happened?"

She hooked one of her legs over one of the lower branches and, though the moustached man was really shouting now, she climbed up so she was next to Timi and Bisi.

She looked over at them.

"She's happy with you," his mum said. "That's the most happy I think I've ever seen her."

Timi looked into Bisi's face and spoke hello to her in his mind. But this time, for the first time, he could feel her answering him back. Hello Timi, he thought she said. Mum sidled a little closer to them on the branch.

"I know it's been hard, for all of us, getting used to our new family," Mum said. "We haven't spent enough time all together and I haven't told you enough; how much I love you and how much Bisi loves you too."

"It's OK," Timi said. "I do know that." And then he spoke a truth, a truth he hadn't been able to say aloud: "I've missed you."

As he spoke, Bisi's small hand reached out and planted itself on Timi's chest. She was answering him back once more: I've missed you too.

"And I've missed you," Mum said, reaching out to stroke his cheek. "And all this time, you've been growing this tree. It's incredible."

"We're trying to protect it," Timi said. "We've been trying to look after it."

His mum nodded and he knew that she understood.

"Come on, everyone," she called out to the other parents. "Get up here. Be with us."

Abi's mum came next. Then Mo's dad and mum. Roberta's dad followed on. And then all of the others rushed to join their children in the tree and ,at the very second that the last parent climbed into its branches, a huge creaking sound filled the air.

It roared in Timi's ears and Bisi looked up, looking for where this giant sound was coming from.

The tree had started to grow right in front of them all.

That was the sound they could hear – it was the sound of growth.

Its branches surged upwards and outwards with such force that they burst through the roof of the building.

Everyone ducked as rubble from the hole in the roof fell down, but the leaves of the tree protected anyone from being hit.

Timi looked up, as did everyone, towards the hole in the roof where the new growth of the tree had split it open.

Light streamed into the room from the hole and Timi could see the blue of the sky through it.

Chapter 18

In Timi's memory, they stayed in the tree for a long time. They read books, the piles that had been left behind, and then Roberta's mum had gone to get more. As they read to each other, the tree had grown again, in front of them.

It was only when they received a special decree that because the tree had grown in the way that it had it could not be chopped down and would always be protected, that they left its branches.

The tree stopped growing in the same way after that. It grew like other trees, little by little.

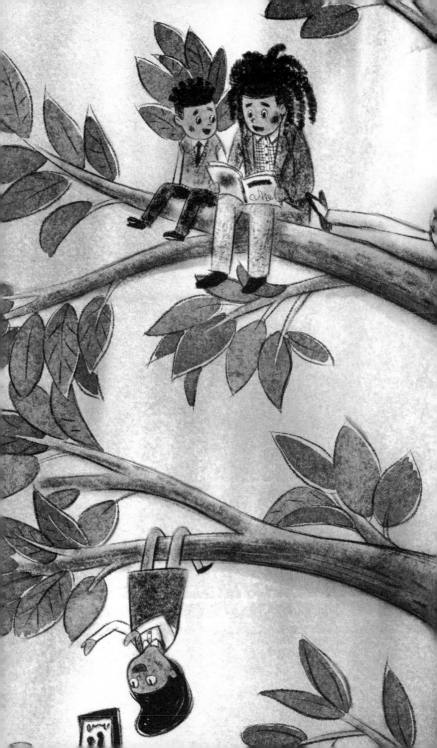

The old library had to be carefully taken down because of the hole in the roof, but there were plans instead to build a special new one around the tree because the tree seemed to like reading so much.

Timi and Bisi would go there every week.

To see the tree, to read books, to be together.

***

"Just like how we're together," she said, burrowing a little further into her Babu's lap.

She had grown heavy from hearing the story. She felt sleepy from listening to the well-told tale.

Her eyes flickered close but, as they did, she looked upwards towards the huge branches of the tree that the library was built around.

Children were reading, sitting in twos or threes, on its lower branches. The library had been built by a clever architect (a person who her Babu had told her had the job of designing buildings) with glass walkways, different floors and a very special design that meant it never disturbed the tree.

"Is this the tree?" she said, sleepily, although she already knew the answer. "Is this the tree from the story?"

The leaves of the tree rustled noisily as a gust of wind blew through them. It's like it's speaking to us, the girl thought.

"Yes," her grandfather said very quietly. He picked her up gently so her head could rest upon his shoulder.

Her eyes flickered close and then opened just once more. She glimpsed the tree again, full of children reading, just like Timi had seen in the story.

As she slipped into sleep she heard her grandfather say, in a whisper: "That's the tree and this is the library, and this is me who grew the tree. And now you can be here. And one day, if you need to, you can grow your own tree."

Acknowledgements

I couldn't be more delighted to be bringing Timi's story to book-life with the incredible team at Knights Of. Hugest thanks to Eishar Brar, Aimée Felone, David Stevens, Marssaié, Danielle Shaw and Tia Ajala.

My gratitude for my agent Clare Wallace is as far-reaching as the branches of Timi's tree. Biggest thanks to all the team at Darley Anderson, especially Mary Darby, Lydia Silver, Kristina Egan, Georgia Fuller, Sheila David, Rosanna Bellingham and Chloe Davis.

Thank you to Sojung Kim-McCarthy for creating illustrations that are full of wonder, magic and hope.

To Dan and B, thank you for sitting in trees with me and helping me to dream and make.

Polly
Ho-Yen

AUTHOR

Polly Ho-Yen used to be a primary school teacher in London and while she was teaching there she would get up very early in the morning to write stories. The first of those stories became her critically acclaimed debut novel BOY IN THE TOWER, which was shortlisted for the Waterstones Children's Book Prize and the Blue Peter Book Award. She lives in Bristol with her husband and daughter.

Sojung Kim-McCarthy

ILLUSTRATOR

Sojung Kim-McCarthy is an award-winning illustrator who loves drawing children in all shapes, sizes and colours. She worked as a designer for a children's magazine as well as an art and design educator in Korea. After moving to Bournemouth to study illustration, she stayed in the seaside town and has been drawing and writing stories of children who feel a little bit different from other people. Sojung loves growing plants from seeds she found in her fruits, and her favourite plant in her windowsill garden at the moment is an avocado tree.

KNIGHTS OF

KNIGHTS OF is a multi award-winning inclusive publisher focused on bringing underrepresented voices to the forefront of commercial children's publishing. With a team led by women of colour, and an unwavering focus on their intended readership for each book, Knights Of works to engage with gatekeepers across the industry, including booksellers, teachers and librarians, and supports non-traditional community spaces with events, outreach, marketing and partnerships.